THE Berenstain BEAR SCOUTS

and the
Run-Amuck Robot

THE *Berenstain* BEAR SCOUTS
and the
Run-Amuck Robot

by Stan & Jan Berenstain
Illustrated by Michael Berenstain

A
LITTLE APPLE
PAPERBACK

SCHOLASTIC INC.
New York Toronto London Auckland Sydney

ISBN 0-590-94477-0

Copyright © 1997 by Berenstain Enterprises, Inc.
All rights reserved. Published by Scholastic Inc.
APPLE PAPERBACKS and the APPLE PAPERBACKS logo are
trademarks and/or registered trademarks of Scholastic Inc.

12 11 10 9 8 7 6 5 4 3   7 8 9/9 0 1 2/0

Printed in the U.S.A.

First Scholastic printing, September 1997

• Table of Contents •

and the
Run-Amuck Robot

• Chapter 1 •

"I Say, Young Chaps! I Say!"

The Bear Scouts were headed for their secret chicken coop clubhouse at the far edge of Farmer Ben's farm. They usually went across Ben's cow pasture. But it was such a nice day they decided to take the long-cut around Squire Grizzly's estate.

The squire was the richest bear in Bear Country, and his estate looked the part. It was a beautiful place, with lovely gardens, handsome statues, and sparkling fountains. And, of course, there was the great mansion itself.

1

As the scouts passed the long curving driveway, they heard someone calling.

"I say, young chaps! I say!"

The voice was familiar, but they couldn't place it until they turned and saw Greeves, the squire's butler. He was running down the driveway, waving and shouting. But Greeves wasn't built for running. His big belly was covering at least as much distance bouncing up and down as its owner was moving forward.

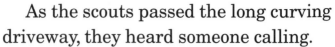

"I — I — say, young chaps! I — I — say!" called Greeves. He was almost out of breath.

"Come on!" said Brother. "Let's meet him halfway. Greeves isn't built for that kind of work."

The scouts changed course and zipped up the driveway. When Greeves saw them coming, he stopped and sat on the curb. He was still trying to catch his breath when the scouts reached him.

"Easy, Greeves, easy," said Brother.

"It's okay," said Sister. "Just wait till you catch your breath." Scouts Lizzy and Fred nodded in agreement.

"Er, what did you want to see us about, Greeves?" asked Brother.

"Oh, it's not I who wishes to see you, young sir," said Greeves. "It's *Lady Grizzly* who wishes to see you."

The scouts looked at each other. Then they looked back at Greeves, who had stood up and was looking almost like his dignified self again.

"Lady Grizzly wants to see *us*?" said Brother.

The scouts did quite a lot of face-making and shrugging as they followed Greeves up the driveway to the massive front doors of the mansion. What could Lady Grizzly possibly want with them?

• Chapter 2 •

Trouble at the Bearsonian?

The Bear Scouts had been inside Grizzly Mansion before. They had come with Papa Q. Bear, Brother and Sister's dad. Papa was just about the finest furniture- and cabinetmaker in Beartown. He did a lot of work for the squire — mostly on Lady Grizzly's collection of priceless antiques. That's how the scouts knew Greeves. They had come with Papa on pickups and deliveries. But they had never come in the front door before. Nor had they ever met Lady Grizzly face-to-face.

The scouts followed Greeves into the

entrance hall. While they gawked at the great chandelier and the portraits of Grizzly ancestors, Greeves opened the double doors that led to the living room. Then he stood just inside them the way butlers do in the movies and said, "The Bear Scouts to see you, mum." The scouts figured they were supposed to go in, so they did.

Lady Grizzly greeted them warmly. "So good to see you," she said. She shook hands with each scout. "Greeves," she said. "Please send Millie in with the tea things.

"Be seated, my dears," continued Lady Grizzly, pointing to an antique table surrounded by five antique chairs. "Ah, yes. Here's Millie with the tea things."

Millie set a large silver tray on the table. There were fancy china cups and saucers, a silver teapot, and a stack of dessert dishes on the tray. At its center was a dish of tea cakes. They were frosted with pink, white, and chocolate icing. Atop each cake was a nutmeat. There were almonds on the pink ones, walnuts on the white ones, and pecans on the chocolate ones. They looked delicious.

"Oh, dear," said Lady Grizzly as she began to pour. "It just occurred to me. You might prefer milk."

"That's okay, ma'am," said Brother. "We're all allowed to drink tea on special occasions."

"Would you prefer lemon or sugar with your tea?" As the scouts said which, Lady Grizzly placed a wedge of lemon on a saucer or plunked a sugar cube into a cup.

The scouts were out of their minds with curiosity about why Lady Grizzly wanted to see them.

"Er, Lady Grizzly," said Brother, "was there something special you wanted to see us about?"

"Oh, yes. Something very special indeed," said Lady Grizzly. "Correct me if I'm wrong, but it's my understanding that you are friendly with Professor Actual Factual, director of the Bearsonian Institution."

"That's right," said Brother.

"And that you are quite fond of him."

"Quite fond," said Brother.

"And," continued Lady Grizzly, "you would be willing to help him in any way you could?"

"Oh, yes," said Brother. "We'd do just about anything to help the professor."

"Good. Then it's settled," said Lady Grizzly. "You're to report to the Bearsonian as junior docents tomorrow morning."

"Junior *who*-cents?" said Sister.

"The Bearsonian opens at nine. I'll pick you up in my limo at eight-thirty. Now, if you'll excuse me, I've things to attend to."

The scouts had all kinds of questions. But their mouths were so full of pink, white, and chocolate cake, they couldn't ask them.

"Greeves," said Lady Grizzly. "Would you please see our friends out?"

Before the scouts quite knew what was happening, that's where they were: out.

"Docent?" said Brother. "What the heck's a docent?"

"*Docent,*" said Fred, who read the dictionary just for fun, "pronounced *DŌ-sent: A guide or lecturer at a museum or university.*"

"Does anybody have any idea what's going on with Lady Grizzly?" asked Brother.

"Knock-knock," said Sister.

"Who's there?" said Lizzy.

"Docent," said Sister.

"Docent who?" said Fred.

"I docent think Lady Grizzly is telling us everything she knows," said Sister.

As the scouts left the Grizzly estate, they were convinced of two things. One, something mysterious was going on at the Bearsonian. And two, they'd better show up at Eagle Road the next morning and find out what the heck it was.

• Chapter 3 •

Mysteriouser and Mysteriouser

The fact that the next day was born in a thick fog just added to the mystery. As the scouts waited at Eagle Road, questions rose with the fog. Was Professor Actual Factual in trouble? If so, what sort of trouble? If the professor wanted them to be junior docents, why didn't he just ask them? True, the scouts hadn't been to see the professor in quite a while. The professor had done so much for them that they couldn't help feeling a little guilty about that.

They heard Lady Grizzly's limo before they saw it. The huge eggplant-colored car appeared out of the fog like a purple ghost. It slowed to a stop. Fitch, the chauffeur, got out. He opened the door for the scouts.

But wait! It wasn't Fitch. It was Greeves wearing a chauffeur's cap. Was it simply that Fitch had the day off? Or was there more to it than that? Mystery was piling onto mystery.

Lady Grizzly gave the scouts a little smile. But that was all. She seemed lost in a fog of thought at least as thick as the one they were driving through.

By the time they neared the Bearsonian, the ground-hugging fog had begun to burn off. The museum's great towers and turrets could be seen, but the rest of the enormous building was still shrouded in fog.

As the limo pulled into the parking lot, they heard a loud banging sound. Peering through the fog, the scouts saw a straw-hatted figure banging on the door of the Bearsonian with his cane. It was Ralph Ripoff. His bright green plaid suit shone through the fog.

What was Bear Country's leading crook and swindler doing banging on the door of the Bearsonian at opening time?

The BEARSONIAN INSTITUTION

"Good morning, Ralph," said Brother. "What are *you* doing here?"

"Well," said Ralph. "If it isn't my little chumps — or, chums — the Bear Scouts. Not that it's any of your business, but I'm doing what you should be doing: protesting this outrage."

The scouts looked around for an outrage. They didn't see any.

"What outrage is that, Ralph?" asked Brother.

"*This* outrage," said Ralph, pointing to the door.

It was the kind of door with a window. Covering the glass on the inside was a sign. It said:

CLOSED UNTIL FURTHER NOTICE

• Chapter 4 •

The Eye in the Window

The scouts had to admit that Ralph had a point. The Bearsonian was a public museum, and it was supposed to be open to the public — even to a crook like Ralph.

"It doesn't make any sense," said Fred.

"It doesn't make any dollars *or* sense," said Ralph. "This is a public institution supported by taxes . . ."

Ralph stopped in midsentence. He hadn't seen Lady Grizzly. But now the fog was lifting.

"Why, Lady Grizzly," said Ralph. "I have

admired you, lo these many years. I can't tell you what a rare pleasure this is."

Nobody ever said Ralph wasn't a smoothie — especially with the ladies. The scouts watched as Ralph went into action. In one smooth motion, Ralph doffed his hat, placed it under his arm along with his cane, took Lady Grizzly's hand, and kissed it. And while he was still bent over, he fished a jeweler's glass out of his pocket, placed it in his eye, and looked closely at the huge ring on Lady Grizzly's finger.

"What a beautiful emerald, my lady. As rare a jewel as yourself."

Lady Grizzly blushed as Ralph straightened up and put his hat back on.

"I'd say that emerald is about seventeen carats," said Ralph.

"Seventeen and a half, actually," said Lady Grizzly.

"My dear lady, as much as I hate to

leave your charming company, I must. But I would add that it's a sad day when a citizen can't enter the Bearsonian and do a little dinosaur research."

"Dinosaur research?" chorused the scouts.

"Yes," said Ralph. "I'm working on a new theory of how dinosaurs became extinct. Well, ta-ta!"

Ralph tipped his hat, and off he went, twirling his cane.

"You're the one who ought to be extinct, Ralph!" shouted Sister.

"Why are you being rude to that charming gentleman?" asked Lady Grizzly.

"'Charming gentleman'?" said Fred. "That's Ralph Ripoff, the biggest crook in Bear Country."

"You mean," said Lady Grizzly, "that Mr. Ripoff is not entirely honest?"

"Lady Grizzly," said Brother, "Ralph is as dishonest as the day is long on the longest day of the year."

"And you don't believe he was here to do research on dinosaurs?" asked Lady Grizzly.

"No," said Lizzy. "But he was here to do research on something just as old: the Bearsonian's gem collection. It's worth zillions, and Ralph's been after it for years."

"What a shame," said Lady Grizzly. "Such a charming fellow. But, as you can see, the professor is behaving rather badly. He's got no business closing down the Bearsonian like this. I mean, it's Bear Country's most important museum. Bears come from all over to visit it."

"Maybe the professor's just off on one of his research projects," said Fred.

"'Wild goose chases' is what the squire calls them," said Lady Grizzly.

"As a matter of fact," said Lizzy, who was into nature, "the professor has done some important research on wild geese."

"I know that, and I'm a big fan of the professor's," said Lady Grizzly. "It's my husband, Squire Grizzly, who's the problem. He's head of the museum's board of directors, and he's got some real problems with the way the professor's running the museum."

"Look," said Brother. "Maybe the professor's got a good reason for closing down the museum. What we've got to do is ask him. Let's find out if he's here. We'll drive around back and check the sciencemobile. If the sciencemobile's here, then so is the professor."

As the Bear Scouts and Lady Grizzly headed for the waiting limo, a corner of the "Closed until further notice" sign was lifted and an eye peered out. It looked like the eye of Professor Actual Factual — except that it had a strange, wild look.

• Chapter 5 •

"Pssst!"

"The professor's got to be inside the museum," said Brother when they reached the rear of the building. "There's the sciencemobile in its regular spot."

"And there's Saucer One in its hangar," said Fred.

The sciencemobile was a white van that the professor fitted out for fieldwork. It had digging tools for fossil hunting, diving gear for marine study, and a minilab for doing tests. It even had a telescope built into its roof to study the stars. Saucer One

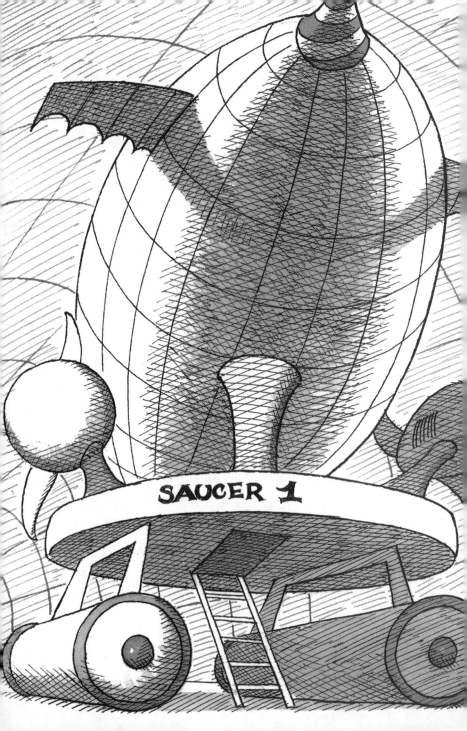

was a combination plane, blimp, and sub-
marine. It was used to fight pollution.

The Bear Scouts and Lady Grizzly
stood in the hangar and looked up at the
great craft.

"You see," said Brother, "the professor is not only a great scientist, he's a great inventor."

"Yes," said Lady Grizzly. "But why has he closed the museum until further notice?"

That's when a piercing "Pssst!" was heard.

"Did you hear a loud 'pssst!'?" said Sister.

It was followed by an equally loud "Bear Scouts! Bear Scouts! Over here!"

The scouts scanned the museum. There were lots of doors. But one of them was half open. Behind the door was a shadowy figure.

It was the professor, of course. He hurried them into the museum, then led them down some steps to a small basement room that the scouts had never seen before. Nor had they ever seen the professor

looking or acting so strangely. His eyes had a wild look. His tweed knicker suit, usually as neat as a pin, was badly smudged and wrinkled. And were those *burn marks* on his sleeves?

But Lady Grizzly had come to read Actual Factual the riot act, and that's what she did. "Professor," she said. "The Bearsonian is a public institution. You have no business closing it down. I'll be very frank. Squire Grizzly is *very upset* with you. You don't return his phone calls. You don't even answer his letters. If you don't mend your ways, I'm very much afraid that the 'Closed until further notice' sign will be changed to read, 'Under new management'."

The professor slumped under Lady Grizzly's attack. He was about to answer when Grizzly Gus, his helper, appeared at the doorway.

"It's time to prepare for the tests, pro-fessor," he said.

"Not now," said the professor.

"But, professor," insisted Gus. "All is in readiness!"

"Not now!" said the professor.

Gus was gone. Down some steps from the sound of it.

What sort of tests? wondered the scouts. And did they have anything to do with the strange goings-on at the Bearsonian?

"Alas, Lady Grizzly," said the professor. "What you say is true. I *have* neglected the museum. The reason is that I'm working on a project that is so important that I must not stop. I must press on. I owe it to myself. I owe it to science. I owe it to all bearkind!"

"Professor," said Brother, "are you working on some kind of secret invention? Is that why you've neglected your duties and closed the museum?"

"Guilty as charged," said the professor. "But this is the invention of a lifetime! An invention that will change the nature of life itself!"

Lady Grizzly and the Bear Scouts put their heads together and had a little meeting right then and there.

". . . an invention that will change the course of history! . . ."

"This invention," said Lady Grizzly. "When will it be completed?"

"One cannot say for sure," said the professor. "But it shouldn't be too much longer. Another test or two . . . And then, of course, I shall present it to the world. It will be my gift to bearkind."

"Well," said Lady Grizzly, "the scouts and I have put our heads together and come up with a plan that should satisfy both you and the squire. Do you want to hear it?"

"I'm all ears, madame," said the professor. "All ears, heart, and soul."

• Chapter 6 •

To Spy or Not to Spy

The professor may have been all ears, heart, and soul, but when he heard the plan he knew it wouldn't work. The plan was for the Bear Scouts and Lady Grizzly to reopen the museum while he and Gus finished their secret invention.

He thought the idea of the Bear Scouts serving as junior docents was fine. The Bear Scouts knew the Bearsonian very well — especially Fred, who not only read the dictionary just for fun but the encyclopedia as well. But there was no way the museum could be reopened right away, even with the help of the Bear Scouts.

"Go see for yourselves," said Actual Factual.

The scouts fanned out through the museum. They were discouraged by what they found.

"It's even worse than the professor said," said Brother when they reported back to Lady Grizzly. "Not only does the place need a top-to-bottom cleaning, but some of the exhibits are missing."

"Exhibits missing?" said Lady Grizzly.

"Yes — the tesla coil, for one," said Fred. "That's the big machine that makes lightning."

"And the static electricity machine, too," said Sister.

"That's the one that makes your fur stand on end," said Lizzy.

"Hmm. Things are worse than I ex-

pected," said Lady Grizzly. "And I'm really worried about the professor."

"Me too," said Sister. "He's beginning to look like one of those mad scientists you see in spooky movies."

"Nevertheless," said Lady Grizzly, "I think we should stay with our plan. We just have to beef it up. Here's what we'll do. I'll go back to the mansion and pick up some of my household staff. I'll donate them to the Bearsonian for as long as it takes to clean up the place. Here's what I want you to do: Find out what the professor's up to. Find out about this secret invention of his."

"You mean you want us to spy on our good friend Professor Actual Factual, who trusts us," said Brother.

"Exactly," said Lady Grizzly.

"We'll do it," said Brother.

• Chapter 7 •

Gus's Trail

Lady Grizzly's part of the plan was working out well. After only a couple of days, her staff had the Bearsonian looking almost like a museum again.

But the Bear Scouts were having no success in finding out what the professor was up to. They thought they knew the Bearsonian pretty well. But the professor was nowhere to be found. He had dropped

completely out of sight. The scouts looked in every nook. They searched in every cranny.

"He must be working on that invention *someplace* in the museum," said Brother.

"Yes," said Fred. "In some secret place that only he knows about."

"Wait," said Sister. "Change that to someplace that only he and *Gus* know about."

"Hey, that's right!" said Fred. "Gus has *got* to know. He was the one who said, 'It's time to prepare for the tests' when we were in that spooky little room. Then he went down some steps."

"Do you think we can find that little room?" said Sister.

"I h-h-hope not," said Lizzy.

• Chapter 8 •

Into the Bowels of the Bearsonian

It didn't take the scouts long to find the spooky basement room. But it took them quite a while to get up enough nerve to go down the stairs. The fact that they were winding stairs didn't help. The scouts were huddled at the top of the stairs, trying to look down. But it's just as hard to look down a winding staircase as it is to describe one without moving your hands.

"I'm scared," said Lizzy.

"Why should you be different from the rest of us?" said Brother.

"How do we know the professor is down there?" asked Fred.

"We don't," said Sister. "But we know *something's* down there because that's where Gus went when he said the tests were ready."

"Look, gang," said Brother. "I know it's scary. But we've got to go down there. The professor's done a lot for us. If he's going over the edge, it's up to us to save him from himself."

So, with Brother leading the way, the Bear Scouts started their descent into the bowels of the Bearsonian. Down, down they went. The stairway was dark and narrow. Its stone walls were rough and damp.

"You know something?" said Fred. "I've read up on the Bearsonian. It wasn't built all at once. I bet this part was the oldest . . ."

"Later, Fred," said Brother.

As the stairs wound down, it got darker and darker. But now there was a flickering light and a crackling sound — and a strange smell.

"What's that funny smell?" said Lizzy. "It's kind of familiar."

"It's ozone," said Fred. "It's that smell you get before a storm. It comes from lightning."

The light, the sound, and the smell were getting stronger when suddenly the stairway opened onto a vast dungeonlike room.

What the scouts saw below was so far beyond the wildest mad scientist scene they could ever have imagined that all the Bear Scouts could do was stare in silent shock.

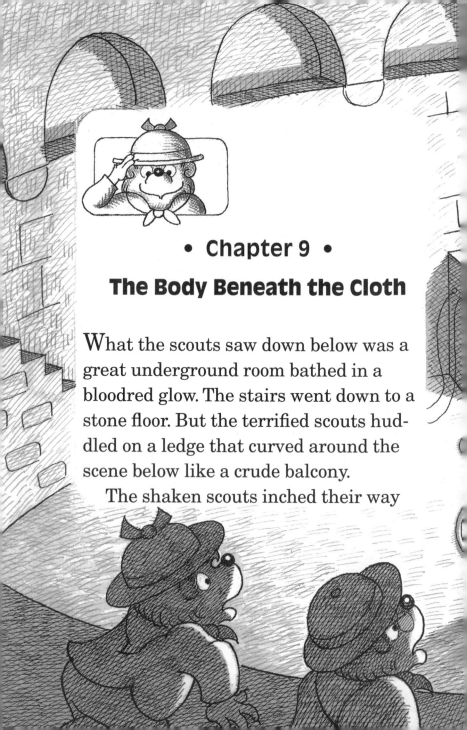

• Chapter 9 •

The Body Beneath the Cloth

What the scouts saw down below was a great underground room bathed in a bloodred glow. The stairs went down to a stone floor. But the terrified scouts huddled on a ledge that curved around the scene below like a crude balcony.

The shaken scouts inched their way

along the ledge and tried to make sense of what they were seeing. The red glow came from a row of lights spaced along the top of a control board that curved around the back wall of the cavernous room. The flashing and the crackling came from a huge coil that stood behind the professor and Gus.

Good grief! It was the missing tesla coil! How did it get down here? They must have taken it apart and brought it down piece by piece.

Oh, yes. The professor and Gus were there, though it was difficult to recognize them in their leather aprons and dark goggles. And there was the missing static electricity machine, too.

But it was the thing that stood before the professor that burned itself into the brains of the terrified Bear Scouts. It was a high table. On it was a body beneath a heavy cloth.

"Look!" hissed Fred.

"I see! I see!" hissed Brother in return.

"What's that clicking noise?" whispered Sister.

"It's — it's — it's my t-t-teeth chattering," said Lizzy.

The professor turned a dial. The crackling got louder. The huge coil began to glow.

"It's just like that old book," said Fred. "The one about Dr. Frankenbear."

"Not now, Fred," said Brother.

"You know," said Fred, "he was the one who wanted to create life. He tried to make a person out of parts of dead bears."

"Please, Fred," said Sister.

"Only it turned out to be a monster with a bolt through its neck," said Fred.

"We know, we know," said Lizzy.

"And he did it with electricity!" said Fred.

The crackling sound was now continuous. The coil glowed red. The stench of ozone filled the air. Gus had begun cranking the handle of the static electricity machine. Now he was cranking it faster and faster. The scouts could feel the electricity in their fur.

The professor gave the big dial another turn. A pale blue tongue of electricity reached out of the glowing coil. Then another turn, and the blue tongue ZAPPED the body beneath the cloth!

Nothing happened. The body beneath the cloth lay perfectly still.

"Thank goodness!" whispered Brother. "Whatever he was trying to do, it didn't work. Come on. Let's get out of here while the getting's good."

The scouts began inching back along the ledge. They simply had to escape from this awful place. But there was some kind of ruckus going on down below. Gus and the professor were arguing. Actual Factual was reaching for the master switch. Gus was trying to stop him.

"No, professor! No!" cried Gus. "You'll fry us all!"

But the professor wouldn't be stopped. He reached up and threw the master switch!

The room went white with a blinding light. Jagged bolts of lightning split the air. *ZAP! ZAP! ZAP!*

And there before the Bear Scouts' very eyes, the body beneath the cloth sat up.

• Chapter 10 •

"Come on Down!"

As amazed as the scouts were by what they'd just seen, they were even more startled by what happened next.

Professor Actual Factual and Gus tore off their aprons and goggles, grasped each other's hands, and danced wildly around the room, hooting and hollering at the top of their lungs.

With his head thrown back, the professor saw the Bear Scouts staring down from the ledge. "Well, bless me if it isn't my friends the Bear Scouts!" he cried. "Delighted to see you! Come on down! I'd like you to meet someone!" With that, he lifted the heavy cloth and put his arm around the shoulders of his latest invention.

Dr. Frankenbear's monster may have had a bolt through its neck. But Professor Actual Factual's monster was *all* bolts — nuts and bolts, that is. Nuts, bolts, gears, wires, batteries, computer chips, steel tubing — everything, as the saying goes, but the kitchen sink. And, perhaps, even some sink parts as well. In other words, Actual Factual's monster wasn't a monster at all. It was a robot — a grinning, lightbulb-eyed, nuts-and-bolts robot.

He was rather bear-shaped in a robotic sort of way, with a squarish head, a tubular muzzle, a great metallic chest, jutting hips, swivel-jointed arms and legs, and clawlike hands and feet.

"Scouts," said the professor, "I'd like you to meet Robow."

"Robow?" said the scouts.

"Yes. It's short for 'robot-of-all-work'." explained the professor.

"Are you saying that Robow can do all different kinds of work?" said Brother.

"That's what I'm saying," said the professor.

"But how can that be?" asked Fred.

"As you can guess," said Actual Factual, "that's a very complicated question. For the time being, let me say that Robow contains more information than the entire contents of the Bear Country Library. He is voice-activated and will respond to any instruction that matches his program. Let me show you.

"Robow," said Actual Factual, "shake hands with and say hello to my friends the Bear Scouts. Be gentle now. This is Scout Brother."

"Hel-lo, Scout Bro-ther," said Robow as he reached down and shook hands with Brother.

"Hello, Robow," said Brother.

As Actual Factual went down the line and introduced the scouts by name, Robow

greeted and shook hands with each scout. As you can guess, the Bear Scouts were really impressed.

"That was very good, Robow," said the professor. "You showed my friends how gentle you can be." Actual Factual picked up a chunk of rock that had broken off the wall. "Now show them how strong you are. Robow, crush this rock."

He placed the rock in Robow's clawlike hand. Robow gripped the rock, then squeezed. It crumbled like a cookie.

"Wow!" said Brother.

"Amazing!" said Fred.

"Awesome!" said Lizzy.

"What's next for Robow?" asked Sister. "What are your plans?"

"Plans are something I have to think about," said the professor. "But what's next is getting Robow up these winding steps."

It turned out to be easier said than

done. When the professor said, "Robow, climb stairs," Robow climbed all right, but he climbed straight ahead.

"No problem," said the professor. "Robow's going to have some gaps and glitches. The fact is, we forgot to program Robow for winding stairs."

The professor and Gus got Robow up the winding staircase, but it took some doing. They managed by saying, "Robow, climb one step and turn right seven degrees," then repeating the instruction over and over. By the time they reached the top, Robow's eyes had begun to flash red.

"Why are Robow's eyes flashing?" asked Lizzy.

"It's just a minor overheating problem," said Actual Factual. "Nothing to worry about."

But the problem Robow had with the winding staircase was just a small hint of the trouble that lay ahead.

• Chapter 11 •

"Professor! Professor! Come Quick!"

Professor Actual Factual was the first to admit that Robow needed work. "But that's to be expected," said the professor. "Most great inventions need work. Thomas Grizzly Edison's first lightbulb blew out after only four minutes. Wilbear and Orville Wright's first airplane flew only one hundred eighty-one feet. BASA's first moon shot fizzled and splashed into Lake Grizzly."

"Nevertheless," said Lady Grizzly, "I wish to propose a toast. To Professor

Actual Factual and his latest and greatest invention. Robow, robot-of-all-work!"

The scouts, the professor, and Lady Grizzly, who were having a juice break in Actual Factual's office, touched paper cups.

They were putting the finishing touches on a plan to present Robow to the world — or, at least, to the leading citizens of Bear Country. The plan included an invitation-only party that would take place the next afternoon in the Bearsonian's grand hall and a press conference that would happen on the museum's front steps. The professor also sent out the following press release:

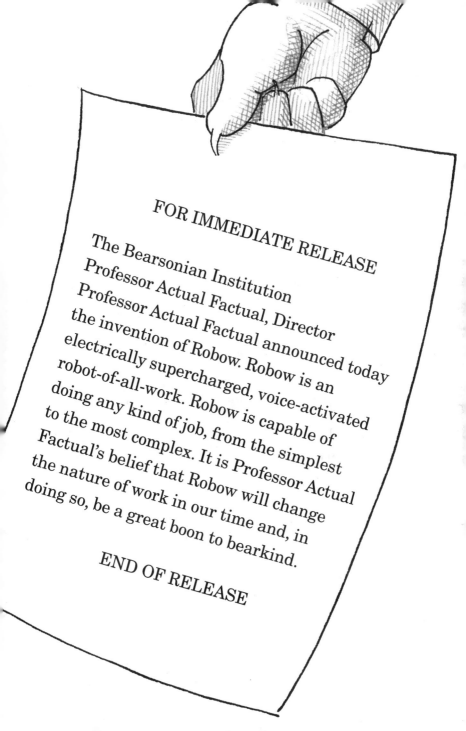

FOR IMMEDIATE RELEASE

The Bearsonian Institution
Professor Actual Factual, Director
Professor Actual Factual announced today
the invention of Robow. Robow is an
electrically supercharged, voice-activated
robot-of-all-work. Robow is capable of
doing any kind of job, from the simplest
to the most complex. It is Professor Actual
Factual's belief that Robow will change
the nature of work in our time and, in
doing so, be a great boon to bearkind.

END OF RELEASE

Meanwhile, Robow was out in the museum, helping Lady Grizzly's staff finish up the big cleanup. Robow had been programmed to answer only to Professor Actual Factual's voiceprint. But there was so much to do that Gus's voiceprint was added to Robow's program. Vacuuming, window washing, and putting out trash

were simple tasks, and Robow did them well. With careful instruction from Gus, Robow even separated the garbage, paper, and recyclable material.

There was still a lot to be done to get ready for tomorrow. The professor was making notes for the press conference, Lady Grizzly was making a last check of the guest list, and the scouts were printing out their junior docent badges on the office computer. It was beginning to look as if it was all going to work when Operation Robow hit an enormous speed bump.

The office door burst open, and Gus rushed in. "Professor! Professor! Come quick!" he cried. "Robow is running amuck in the Hall of Dinosaurs!"

Actual Factual, Lady Grizzly, and the Bear Scouts were out the door faster than you can say, "Tyrannosaurus rex."

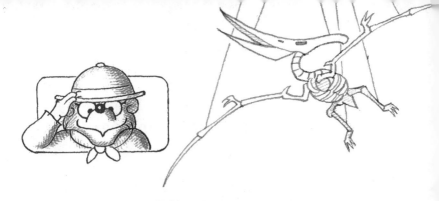

• Chapter 12 •

Robow Mops Up

The Hall of Dinosaurs was at the far end of the museum. What Actual Factual and the others saw when they got there took what was left of their breath away.

Robow was in an attack crouch. His lightbulb eyes were flashing red. He was holding a dinosaur bone as if it were a club. Greeves, Lady Grizzly's butler, and

Millie, her maid, were atop the T-rex skeleton. Other members of her staff had gotten out of harm's way by climbing into the Brontosaurus skeleton's ribcage.

Robow saw the professor and the others. He came toward them, his eyes flashing red and his club at the ready.

"Robow, stop!" said the professor.

That's all it took. The emergency was over. Robow stopped in his tracks. His eyes stopped flashing. The dinosaur bone fell to the floor. All those present breathed a sigh of relief. Greeves, Millie, and the others climbed down from their perches.

"All right, Gus," said the professor. "Tell me, what went wrong?"

"That's the trouble," said Gus. "*Nothing* went wrong. Robow was doing beautifully. I handed him a broom and said, 'Robow, sweep,' and he swept. When the job was done, I said, 'Robow, stop,' and he stopped."

"And then?" said the professor, listening carefully for a clue to what went wrong.

"Then I wrapped a dust cloth around the mop," continued Gus. "I handed it to

Robow and said, 'Robow, remove spider-webs.' He did a beautiful job. He removed every web. Then I said, 'Robow, stop,' and he stopped."

"Yes, and then?" said the professor.

"Then I took the cloth off the mop and said, 'Robow, mop up.' That's when his eyes started flashing and he came after us with the dinosaur bone. I yelled, 'Robow, stop! Robow, stop!' But it didn't do any good. He just went crazy."

The professor thought for a long moment. Then he said, "Robow didn't go crazy. He just chose the wrong definition."

"Wrong definition?" said Lady Grizzly. There was puzzlement all around.

"That's right," said the professor. "Fred, how many definitions are there under 'mop'?"

"Seven," said Fred.

"Within that number, are there any under 'mop up'?" asked the professor.

"Two," said Fred. "*Mop up: to clean an area using a mop.* Also *mop up* (military): *to rid the field of battle of the enemy after a battle.*"

"Hmm," said the professor.

"Hmm what?" said Brother.

"I told you Robow needed work," said the professor.

Later on, Actual Factual and the scouts were in the professor's office, looking back over the events of the day and thinking about the big doings tomorrow. Actual Factual looked worried. So did the scouts.

"Professor," said Brother, "do you think Robow is ready for prime time? Suppose he runs amuck tomorrow when all the big shots are here."

"Robow did not run amuck," said the professor. "He simply chose the wrong definition. He's bound to misunderstand from time to time — especially under stress.

No, there's a much more serious problem: Robow didn't stop when ordered to."

"He stopped when *you* ordered him to," said Lizzy.

"Exactly," said the professor. "And that's the key. Adding Gus's voice to the program was a mistake. It confused Robow. I've got to remove Gus's voice from the program and sharpen my own voiceprint so that Robow answers to me and me alone. There will be a lot of stress tomorrow. Robow will hear a lot of voices. We've got to make sure he doesn't get confused and overheat."

"Professor," said Brother, "how would you like a little insurance so that you can be *sure* Robow will answer to you and you alone?"

"What do you have in mind?" asked the professor.

"Do you remember a game called Simon Says?" said Brother.

"I remember the game," said Actual Factual. "But I don't understand what it has to do with tomorrow."

Brother explained.

That evening the professor did two things. He sharpened his voiceprint and reprogrammed Robow to respond only to instructions that began with the words "Simon says."

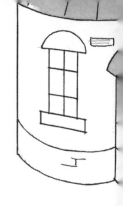

• Chapter 13 •

"Dum-de-dum-dum!"

"Professor, you call your latest invention a robot-of-all-work. Do you mean to suggest that Robow can do any job a bear can do?"

"That's exactly what I meant to suggest," said Actual Factual.

The press conference had drawn a much bigger crowd than expected. Reporters had come from all over Bear Country. There was even a satellite truck from

Big Bear City covering the press conference live. It was being held on the Bearsonian's front steps as planned. Actual
Factual was on the top step with a micro-
phone. Junior docents Brother and Sister
had attached microphones to two of the
professor's fishing poles. They were running from reporter to reporter as the questions came fast and thick.

"Professor, do you seriously mean *all*
work?"

"I do indeed," said the professor.

"No matter how difficult or complex?"

"That's right," said the professor. "No
matter how difficult or complex."

That really got the reporters going.
Brother and Sister had a hard time keep-
ing up with the questions.

"Could Robow build a house, professor?"

"Pilot a jet?"

"Fly a rocket to the moon?"

"Perform brain surgery?"

"Yes, yes, yes, and yes," said the professor.

"Could Robow be a reporter?"

"In his sleep," said the professor. That got a nervous titter from the audience of reporters.

"I have a rather more serious question, professor."

"I'll be happy to answer it," said Actual Factual.

"Sir, your release says — and I quote — 'It is the professor's belief that Robow will change the nature of work in our time.' Now here's my question: If we're going to have all these Robows doing all the work, what are *we* going to be doing? Twiddling our thumbs, contemplating our navels?"

"Those who wish to twiddle will twiddle. Those who wish to contemplate will contemplate," said the professor. "But others will be free to seek the higher meaning of life, to listen to the music of the spheres, to promote the brotherhood of bears. But you must excuse me. I see that my guests are arriving."

Automobiles plain and fancy were pulling into the museum's parking lot. There were a number of limousines in the mix, including Squire Grizzly's. Lady Grizzly was already inside. She and junior

docents Fred and Lizzy were setting up the punch table. Robow was inside, too, in a quiet room.

Some guests were arriving on foot.

"Uh-oh," said Brother. "I think I see a party crasher."

It was Ralph Ripoff, grinning and twirling his cane to beat the band.

Sister had a copy of the guest list. "No," she said. "Lady Grizzly put him on the list."

"*Dum*-de-dum-dum!" said Brother.

• Chapter 14 •
Let's Party!

The plan that Actual Factual had worked out with Lady Grizzly and junior docents Brother, Sister, Fred, and Lizzy was for Robow to greet the guests as they arrived and then mix among them. All with Actual Factual standing close by, of course.

The greeting part was working beautifully. The professor had programmed Robow with random greetings, so he said different words to each guest. He'd say, "How do you do?" to one guest, "Pleased to meet you" to another, and "Delighted to make your acquaintance" to still another. The guests were very impressed. It made Robow seem almost like a real person.

"Hey, that Robow is quite a fellow," said Farmer Ben. "I wonder if he can slop hogs."

"I think he can," said junior docent Sister. "Would you and Mrs. Ben like some punch?"

"Thankee. Don't mind if we do," said Ben.

"You know, sis," said Brother, "That's the first time I ever saw Farmer Ben wearing a jacket."

"And probably the last," said Sister.

Squire Grizzly wasn't as impressed with Robow's friendly greeting — "How-do-you-do-sir-it's-a-pleasure-to-meet-you" — as he was by the idea of using Robows as factory workers.

"That Robow could do the work of five of my regular workers," said Squire Grizzly.

"Hey, look!" said Sister. "Robow's dancing with Lady Grizzly!"

"What's that crazy dance they're doing?" said Brother. "Uh-oh, Robow's eyes are starting to flash red!"

"It's called the jitterbug," said Gramps. "It's a dance we used to do when we were young."

"Oh, my goodness!" cried Gran. "He's going to throw her over his back! Somebody do something!"

"Stop, Robow! Stop!" cried the professor. Luckily, junior docent Fred was there

to remind the professor to say, "*Simon says* stop!"

"Thank-you-for-the-dance-ma'am," said Robow.

"Oh, you're welcome, Robow," said Lady Grizzly, trying to put herself back together.

"Hey, Robow!" someone shouted. "Let's see you do a little tango!" Someone else shouted, "How about a little cha-cha-cha!"

Robow knew all those dances. So it was a good thing the professor had sharpened his voiceprint. Brother's "Simon says" idea was working, too. Except that, as anybody who has ever played Simon Says knows, sometimes you forget to say "Simon says."

"That Robow's a heckuva dancer," said Papa Bear. "But why are his eyes flashing red like that?"

"He's just overheating a little," said Brother. "Professor, don't you think you should start giving Robow some easier jobs?"

"Good thinking, Brother," said the professor. He saw that Mayor and Mrs. Honeypot had just arrived and were right beside the checkroom. He turned to the robot and said, "Robow, go greet — er, *Simon says* go greet Mayor and Mrs. Honeypot and then check their coats."

The professor relaxed when he saw that Robow's eyes had stopped flashing. But the next thing he knew was that Mayor Honeypot, who sometimes got the fronts and backs of his words mixed up, was shouting at him.

"Soo dumthing — er, do something!" cried the mayor. "That rool fobot — er, fool robot, is destroying our coats!"

"Stop that! Stop that!" cried the professor. By the time he remembered to say, "*Simon says* stop that!" Robow had taken a black crayon and made check marks all over Mayor and Mrs. Honeypot's coats.

"Too bad about the mayor and his Mrs.," said Chief of Police Bruno as the Honeypots stormed out of the museum. "But that Robow character would make a heckuva security guard."

"Speaking of security, professor," said Brother, "I just saw Ralph Ripoff sneak into the Hall of Gems!"

Actual Factual knew what that meant. He neither hesitated nor forgot to say "Simon says."

"*Simon says* seize Ralph Ripoff! Green suit!" cried the professor.

Robow stalked into the darkened Hall of Gems. The sounds of a struggle! Screams and cries for help! The professor and the Bear Scouts rushed in and turned on the light.

The gems were safe in their cases. Ralph, however, was not. He was down to his underwear and in the steely grip of Robow, who had torn off most of Ralph's clothes.

"*Simon says* stop!" cried the professor.

Robow stopped. But his eyes were flashing dangerously. Ralph, of course, was in a sputtering rage.

• Chapter 15 •

Overexposed

"You're under arrest, Ralph," said Chief Bruno. "Come with me."

"Under arrest?" cried Ralph. "What's the charge?"

"Indecent exposure," said the chief.

"I'm grateful that Robow saved the gem collection," said the professor. "But I don't understand why he tore off Ralph's clothes."

"I think I do," said Fred. "You told Robow, 'Seize Ralph Ripoff! Green suit!' Robow *thought* you said, 'Seize Ralph! Rip off green suit!'"

"Well, at least the gems are safe," said the professor.

"Yes," said Gus, who had joined the group. "But Robow is not. He's overheating badly."

"What do you suggest?" said the professor.

"The party's breaking up, anyway," said Gus. "Let's just leave him in here to cool down."

"Agreed," said the professor.

Robow's eyes were still flashing red when they turned out the light in the Hall of Gems and closed the door behind them. That was the last time anyone saw Robow while he was still in one piece.

• Chapter 16 •

An Idea Whose Time Has Come?

They heard it while they were saying their good-byes to Squire and Lady Grizzly. It sounded like a string of firecrackers. But the sound was covered by the buzz of the party breaking up.

"Professor, I want to thank you for a most excellent afternoon," said Squire Grizzly. "Glad to see the museum in such tip-top shape. Interesting chap, that Robow. I can see a whole line of 'em hard at work making more Robows. They'd make fine workers. No coffee breaks. Work twenty-four hours a day. I tell you, professor, it's an idea whose time has come!"

"Thank you, squire," said Actual Factual. "It was good of you to come — and many heartfelt thanks to you, Lady Grizzly."

The Grizzlys were the last to leave. Actual Factual, the Bear Scouts, and Gus rushed into the Hall of Gems and turned on the light.

There lay Robow, a smoking pile of nuts, bolts, wires, computer chips, and sink parts.

"Gee, we're sorry," said Brother, looking at the sad sight. The rest of the troop mumbled its regrets.

"There's no need to be sorry," said the professor. "The only regret I have about Robow One is that I didn't do a better job on the overheating problem. That can be easily corrected."

"You said 'Robow One,'" said Sister. "Does that mean there's going to be a Robow Two?"

Actual Factual smiled. "Do you think there should be?" he asked.

"Gee, we don't know," said Brother. "You're the inventor."

"That's right," said the professor with a small smile. He turned to Gus. "Would you take care of what's left of Robow? You know what to do. Come on, scouts. Let's get some air. We can look at the sunset."

The Bear Scouts and the professor sat

on the front steps of the Bearsonian and looked out over Bear Country. They could see Farmer Ben's farm and, beyond that, the Bear family's tree house. Off to the left was busy Beartown, with its stores, schools, and factories.

"You know something, professor?"

"I will if you tell me," said Actual Factual.

"Well, I've been thinking," said Brother. "You know, about work and all. Take Farmer Ben, for instance. He *likes* to slop hogs and feed the chickens and ride on that big old tractor of his."

"Yes," said the professor. "I suppose he does."

"The same with my dad," said Sister. "He *likes* working with wood. Sawing and hammering and all. And Dr. Gert, too. She *likes* being a doctor and taking care of folks."

"The same with Chief Bruno," said Fred. "He *likes* catching crooks."

"And don't forget Ralph Ripoff," said Lizzy. "He *likes* swindling and cheating."

"And how about you, professor?" said Sister. "You *like* science and inventing and stuff."

"I've been thinking, too," said Actual Factual. "And the answer to your question is that there's not going to be a Robow Two. Come on. Let's go pay our respects to Robow One."

The scouts hadn't noticed, but Gus was out in the field in front of the museum. He was digging a hole. He had a sign and a plastic bag filled with nuts and bolts.

"It's double-thick plastic to prevent pollution," explained the professor.

Gus lowered the plastic bag into the hole and covered it with earth. The little group looked at the sunset, then turned and went back to the Bearsonian. All that was left of Robow was a mound of earth and a sign that said:

HERE LIES ROBOW.
AN IDEA WHOSE TIME
HADN'T QUITE COME.

• About the Authors •

Stan and Jan Berenstain have been writing and illustrating books about bears for more than thirty years. Their very first book about the Bear Scout characters was published in 1967. Through the years the Bear Scouts have done their best to defend the weak, catch the crooked, joust against the unjust, and rally against rottenness of all kinds. In fact, the scouts have done such a great job of living up to the Bear Scout Oath, the authors say, that "they deserve a series of their own."

Stan and Jan Berenstain live in Bucks County, Pennsylvania. They have two sons, Michael and Leo, and four grandchildren. Michael is an artist, and Leo is a writer. Michael did the pictures in this book.

Don't Miss

THE Berenstain BEAR SCOUTS

and the Ice Monster

"After him!" cried Papa. "Let's show him what doomsday's all about!"

The monster took one look at all those rocks, boards, and clubs and shambled away.

"Look!" cried Scout Fred. "He's heading for the ice tower!"

"Good grief!" cried Brother. "He's climbing the ice tower!"

It was quite a scene: the hideous, big-as-a-house ice monster climbing the great ice tower, the crazed crowd gathered at its base waving its weapons. The noisy arrival of Chief Bruno and Officer Marguerite on snowmobiles just added to the confusion.

"We've got a monster problem, Chief," said Papa. "But I've got an idea. There's only one individual who can go up against that monster, and that's Bigpaw! Let me borrow one of your snowmobiles and I'll fetch him."

"But Bigpaw's hibernating," protested Sister. "There's no telling what'll happen if you try to wake a hibernating bear — especially a bear as big and powerful as Bigpaw!"

"I'll just have to take that chance," cried Papa. He hopped onto the snowmobile and roared off toward the mountains.